1935 ...

read a good book, you needed
either a lot of money or a library card.
Cheap paperbacks were available, but their
poor production generally mirrored the quality
between the covers. One weekend that year,
Allen Lane, Managing Director of The Bodley Head,
having spent the weekend visiting Agatha Christie,
found himself on a platform at Exeter station trying to
find something to read for his journey back to London.
He was appalled by the quality of the material he had to
choose from. Everything that Allen Lane achieved from that
day until his death in 1970 was based on a passionate belief
in the existence of 'a vast reading public for *intelligent*
books at a low price'. The result of his momentous vision
was the birth not only of Penguin, but of the 'paperback
revolution'. Quality writing became available for the price of
a packet of cigarettes, literature became a mass medium
for the first time, a nation of book-borrowers became a
nation of book-buyers – and the very concept of book
publishing was changed for ever. Those founding
principles – of quality and value, with an overarching
belief in the fundamental importance of reading –
have guided everything the company has
done since 1935. Sir Allen Lane's
pioneering spirit is still very much alive
at Penguin in 2005. Here's to
the next 70 years!

MORE THAN A BUSINESS

'We decided it was time to end the almost customary half-hearted manner in which cheap editions were produced – as though the only people who could possibly want cheap editions must belong to a lower order of intelligence. We, however, believed in the existence in this country of a vast reading public for intelligent books at a low price, and staked everything on it'
Sir Allen Lane, 1902–1970

'The Penguin Books are splendid value for sixpence, so splendid that if other publishers had any sense they would combine against them and suppress them'
George Orwell

'More than a business … a national cultural asset'
Guardian

'When you look at the whole Penguin achievement you know that it constitutes, in action, one of the more democratic successes of our recent social history'
Richard Hoggart

The Worst Thing a Suburban Girl Could Imagine

MELISSA BANK

PENGUIN BOOKS

PENGUIN BOOKS

Published by the Penguin Group
Penguin Books Ltd, 80 Strand, London WC2R 0RL, England
Penguin Group (USA) Inc., 375 Hudson Street, New York, New York 10014, USA
Penguin Group (Canada), 10 Alcorn Avenue, Toronto, Ontario, Canada M4V 3B2
(a division of Pearson Penguin Canada Inc.)
Penguin Ireland, 25 St Stephen's Green, Dublin 2, Ireland
(a division of Penguin Books Ltd)
Penguin Group (Australia), 250 Camberwell Road, Camberwell, Victoria 3124,
Australia (a division of Pearson Australia Group Pty Ltd)
Penguin Books India Pvt Ltd, 11 Community Centre,
Panchsheel Park, New Delhi – 110 017, India
Penguin Group (NZ), cnr Airborne and Rosedale Roads, Albany,
Auckland 1310, New Zealand (a division of Pearson New Zealand Ltd)
Penguin Books (South Africa) (Pty) Ltd, 24 Sturdee Avenue,
Rosebank 2196, South Africa

Penguin Books Ltd, Registered Offices: 80 Strand, London WC2R 0RL, England

www.penguin.com

The Girls' Guide to Hunting and Fishing first published in Great Britain by Viking 1999
Published in Penguin Books 2000
This story published as a Pocket Penguin 2005

1

Set in 10.5/12.5pt Monotype Dante
Typeset by Palimpsest Book Production Limited
Polmont, Stirlingshire
Printed in England by Clays Ltd, St Ives plc

Keep a calm atmosphere and children won't worry.

– From *The Sailor's Handbook*,
Edited by Halsey C. Herreshoff

I

My father knew he had leukemia for years before telling my brother and me. He explained that he hadn't wanted his illness to interfere with our lives. It had barely interfered with his own, he said, until recently. 'I've been very lucky,' he said, and I could tell he wanted us to see it this way, too.

This was an early spring weekend in the suburbs, and the three of us sat outside on the screened-in porch. My mother was in the background that afternoon, doing the brunch dishes and offering more coffee, weeding the garden and filling the bird feeder. It was warm but not hazy the way it can be in spring; the sky was blue with hefty clouds. The dark pink and red azaleas were just beginning to bloom.

Back in New York, I called my father before I left work. He was just getting home from the office. 'Hi, love,' he said. I knew he was in the kitchen, sipping a gin and tonic while my mother cooked dinner. His voice was as strong and reassuring as ever.

I tried to sound normal, too. Busy. When he asked what I was doing that night, I glanced at the newspaper open on my desk –

a writer I'd heard on public radio was reading at a bookstore downtown – and I decided to go, so I could say so to my father.

After we hung up, I stared out of my window into the windows of the office building across the street. This was the year everyone started saying, 'Work smart instead of long,' and the offices were deserted, except for the tiny shapes of cleaning women in their grayish-blue uniforms, one or two on every floor. The woman would go into an office and clean. A second later the light would go out, and she would go on to the next office.

I heard the cleaning woman on my own floor, emptying wastebaskets and moving her custodial cart down the hall.

Her name was Blanca, and she was my social life.

I'd been a rising star at H— until Mimi Howlett, the new executive editor, decided I was just the lights of an airplane.

The week she arrived she took me to lunch. At the restaurant, people turned around. Some knew Mimi and waved, but others just looked at her because she was beautiful enough for them to wonder if she was famous, and she carried herself as though she was.

I couldn't help staring, either – it was like she was a different species from me. She had the lollipop proportions of a model – big head, stick figure – pale skin, wintergreen eyes, and a nose barely big enough to breathe out of. That day, she was wearing a fedora, a charcoal-colored suit with a short jacket and an ankle-length skirt, and delicate laced-up boots. She might've been a romantic heroine from a novel, *The Age of Innocence* maybe, except she was with me, in my sacky wool dress, a worker in a documentary about the lumpen proletariat.

Her voice now: it was soft and whispery, the sound of perfume talking, which made her very occasional use of the word *fuck* as striking and even beautiful as a masculine man expressing nuanced and heartfelt emotion.

She began by telling me how sorry she was about my former

boss, Dorrie, who'd been fired. She did seem sorry, and I hoped she was.

Then we talked about our favorite books – not recently published ones, but what we'd grown up reading and the classics we'd loved in college.

She'd gone to Princeton, she said, and asked where I'd gone. When I told her the name of my tiny college, she said that she thought she'd heard of it, adding, 'I think the sister of a friend of mine went there.'

She didn't mean to be disparaging, which only made me feel worse. Sitting across from her, I remembered all the rejections I'd gotten from colleges with median SAT scores hundreds of points lower than Princeton's. I remembered the thin envelopes, and how bad it felt to tell my father each night at dinner.

Mimi said, 'Are you okay?'

'Yes,' I said. 'Do you mind if I smoke?'

I tried to avoid Mimi. Her presence seemed to call forth every rejection I'd ever experienced – the teachers who'd looked at me as though I held no promise, the boys who didn't like me back. Around her, I became fourteen again.

I doubt my reaction was new to her, but it couldn't have been pleasant. Even so, she tried to be kind and took me under her fluffy white wing.

She brought in lipsticks she no longer wore, silk scarves she thought I'd like. She let me know when a good sale was going on at Bergdorf or Barneys. She told me about an apartment, which my friend Sophie wound up taking.

The first time Mimi asked me to read one of her submissions, she said, 'I thought you might be interested in this.' But soon she was handing me stacks of manuscripts, every submission she didn't want to read herself, a terrible, endless supply. She did it in the nicest possible manner, as though asking a favor I was free to refuse.

Without realizing it, I became less the associate editor I'd been than an assistant she'd decided to bring up. She was forever interrupting herself to explain some basic aspect of publishing to me. I had to stop myself from saying, *Yes, I know*, which would've come across as an unwillingness to learn. And I did seem to know less and less.

After a while, she never seemed to look at me without assessing who I was and what I was capable of becoming. I could tell she doubted my devotion, and in this she was perfectly justified.

That afternoon, she'd held up her bottle of perfume, and I'd brought my wrists forward to be sprayed, as usual. Then she said that an agent had called asking about *Deep South*, a lyrical novel he'd submitted weeks ago – *Did I know anything about it?* I told her I'd look for it.

I knew where it was, of course – under my desk, where I hid all the manuscripts I hadn't read for her. Now I put *Deep South* in my book bag, said good night to Blanca, and headed downtown for the reading.

The bookstore was so crowded that I had to stand along the back shelves. Someone was already up at the microphone welcoming everyone. I was taking off my jacket and folding it over my book bag, when I heard the welcomer say, '. . . his editor, Archie Knox.'

Since we'd broken up, I'd seen Archie a few times at readings and book parties. The first time, I went up to him, but he barely nodded before turning his back on me. My friend Sophie told me that he avoided me because he cared so much, but that wasn't how it felt.

From where I stood, he didn't look older or different. He wore an oatmealy Shetland-wool sweater I knew. He was saying that he'd read the book, *Loony*, straight through, forgetting dinner and postponing bed; he'd stayed up all night and eaten moo shu pork for breakfast, which he did not recommend. He paused and I saw him see me – his eyebrows pulled together – and he coughed and finished his story.

There was applause and then the author, Mickey Lamm, in a brown suit and sneakers, hugged Archie. Mickey looked exactly like his voice: bangs in his eyes and a bouncy walk; puppy-dog tails were what he was made of, though he was probably forty.

When the applause subsided, he said into the microphone, 'Archie Knox, the best editor anywhere,' and he clapped, and got the crowd clapping again with him. He had a crooked smile that didn't quite cover his teeth, and at about ninety words a minute he invited all the aspiring writers in the audience to send their manuscripts to Archie Knox at K—, and he gave the full address, including zip. In an announcer's voice he said, 'That address again . . .' and repeated it.

I couldn't see where Archie was, but I could feel him there. I closed my eyes while Mickey read and pictured Archie holding a pencil above the manuscript.

Loony was a memoir of childhood, and the chapter Mickey read was about stealing pills from his psychiatrist stepfather's medicine cabinet. As it turned out, they were just anti-nauseants, though he and his friends imagined they'd discovered an excellent high – and he kept stealing those pills.

Mickey wasn't reading as much as being the boy he'd been – daring devil, winking leprechaun, smiling sociopath – especially when he got caught stealing, and his stepfather asked, 'Are you nauseated, Mickey?'

In the audience's laughter, I heard Archie's.

I couldn't bear the prospect of him ignoring me. After the applause, I got my stuff together fast. On my way out, I heard someone from the audience ask the standard question *What do you read for inspiration?* and Mickey's answer: 'Bathroom walls.'

*

I was living at my aunt Rita's old apartment in the Village. Legally, I wasn't supposed to be there so I hadn't really moved in. There wasn't room, anyway; no one had moved my aunt's stuff out. It seemed less defined by my presence than her absence, and the little terrace was the only place in it I liked to be.

But I couldn't read out there. So I got myself a tall diet root beer and a coaster, and took *Deep South* to her big formal dining-room table.

The novel started on flora (dark woods, tangled thickets, choking vines) and went to fauna – if bugs counted as fauna. Bugs, bugs, bugs – too small to see or as big as birds, swarms and loners, biting, stinging, and going up your nose. The prose was dense and poetic; it was like reading illegible handwriting, and after a few pages my eyes were just going left to right, word to word, not reading at all. So, when the phone rang, I answered on ring one.

Archie said, 'It's me,' though we'd been broken up for almost two years. 'What's the matter?'

I was too surprised to answer. Then, I started crying and couldn't stop.

Archie hated to hear anyone cry – not because it hurt him or anything like that, he just hated crying. I could tell he was calling from a pay phone and knew that he was probably out to dinner with Mickey and his entourage, but he didn't say. He was silent, waiting for me to talk.

Finally, I got out: 'My dad has leukemia.'

All he said was, 'Oh, honey,' but in it I heard everything I needed to. He told me to blow my nose and come over to dinner the next night.

2

Archie answered the door, wearing the black cashmere sweater I'd given him as a Christmas present. 'Hello, dear,' he said. He sort of patted my shoulder.

6

Behind him I saw peonies on the dining-room table. They were white and edged with magenta, still closed into little fists. 'Oh,' I said. 'My favorite.'

He said, 'Yes, I know,' and his eyes said, *You're not yourself.*

While he poured club soda and squeezed lime into it, he told me that he'd stood over those peonies and asked, ordered, and begged them to open, but they were as resistant as I'd been at the beginning.

'Maybe they're seeing someone else,' I said.

For dinner, we were having soft-shell crabs, another favorite of mine. While he sautéed them, I told him that my father didn't have the leukemia you usually heard about; it wasn't the kind that killed people right away.

'Good,' Archie said.

I said, 'But he's already had it for nine years.'

Archie was setting our plates down on the dining-room table, and he stopped and turned around. 'Nine years?'

I nodded.

We sat. I repeated what my father had said about not wanting the illness to interfere with my life, but I was afraid Archie would suspect what I did, so I said it out loud: 'I think maybe he didn't think I could handle it or help him.'

'No,' Archie said, 'he didn't want to put you through it.' My father had been strong and noble, Archie said, which was how I was trying to see it, too.

I told him that my dad's doctor – Dr. Wischniak – had come over and explained the illness to Henry and me privately. I reminded Archie that I'd barely passed non-college-bound biology, but I understood that the leukemia and chemotherapy had weakened my father's immune system, and he'd become susceptible to infections, like the shingles and pneumonia he'd already had. I told Archie that my brother asked the doctor about the illness and the treatment; red cells and white ones, a bone-marrow transplant and blood transfusions. Then I asked my one question, *How much time does he have?* Dr. Wischniak said he couldn't answer that.

'No idea?' Archie said.

I shook my head.

I said that my question seemed to bother the doctor, and it sounded wrong to me, too, though I didn't understand why. 'I felt like I'd spoken French in science class.'

Archie said, 'Maybe he just didn't like being asked a question he couldn't answer.'

'Maybe,' I said.

We took our coffee into the living room. He stood at the stereo and asked if I had any requests.

'*Something Blue*-ish,' I said.

While he flipped through his records, he told me about the time he'd asked his daughter for requests; she was about three and cranky after a nap, going down the stairs one at a time on her butt. He imitated her saying, 'No music, Daddy.'

'I told her we had to listen to something,' he said. 'And she languorously put her hair on top of her head and like a world-weary nightclub singer said, "Coltrane then."'

That's what he put on now. I asked how Elizabeth was, and he said she was beautiful and smart and impressive, finishing her junior year at Stanford. She'd spent the year in Israel on a kibbutz. She'd forgiven him, he said, and they'd grown close; he might meet her in Greece over the summer.

I said that I'd been hoping to go to Greece that summer myself, but I wasn't sure now.

He sat beside me on the sofa, and patted my hand.

When we talked about Mickey's reading, I admitted that I hadn't read *Loony* yet, and Archie promised to get a copy to me. I could see how proud he was of the book, and I was wondering if I'd ever felt that way or would, when he asked what I'd acquired recently.

'Malaise,' I said. I wasn't ready to pinpoint how nowhere my career was. 'I have a new boss,' I said.

'Who's that?'

I said, 'Mimi Howlett.'

He said, 'I knew Mimi when she was an editorial assistant,' and right away I thought, *He slept with her*.

He asked me what the last book I loved was. I was trying to remember the title of any book I'd read recently, when he added, as though it was just another bit of conversation, 'Did you read my book?'

'Yes,' I said.

'Did you like it?'

'A lot,' I said.

He asked if I minded that he'd written a novel about us, and I said, 'I minded the way you submitted it to my publisher.'

'It was a mistake,' he said. 'I'm sorry.'

'I know,' I said.

He said, 'I was a little bit desperate.'

'Can you be "a little bit desperate"?' I asked. 'Isn't that like being "a trifle horrified"? Or "mildly ecstatic"?'

'Leave a man his dignity,' he said.

I said, 'The amazing thing was that you pulled off a happy ending.'

He said, 'We deserved it.'

'How're you doing on the drinking?' I asked.

He said, 'Great,' and told me that he'd started taking a drug called Antabuse, which would make him violently ill if he drank. Plus, he'd been to AA. He showed me a white poker chip they'd given him to mark his sobriety. He said he didn't go to the meetings, but he carried the chip around in his pocket all day.

I told him I was happy for him. Then I said, 'What do you think they give away at Gamblers Anonymous?'

When he hugged me good night, it was just arms and

9

squeezing, but now the familiar lack of comfort comforted me. I'd once told him that his hugging reminded me of the surrogate wire mothers in the rhesus-monkey experiment; it was more like the idea of a hug than the real thing.

'Archie,' I said, 'your hugging has not improved.'

He said, 'Lack of practice.'

He called the next day and asked if I wanted to have dinner.

I confessed that I was criminally behind in my submissions and planned to read my head off.

'Bring them here,' he said. 'And I'll read my head off, too.'

I called home before leaving the office. It was a relief not to pretend to be busy. 'You sound good,' my father said, and I could hear how pleased he was.

I sat in Archie's big leather armchair. He stretched out on the sofa. When I started to say something, he said, 'No talking in the library,' and reminded me that I was there to work.

After a while, he said that he was ordering Chinese, which he called *Chinois*, and what did I want?

I said a librarian's 'Sh.'

He called and ordered – he knew what I liked, anyway – and when our dinner arrived and we set the dining-room table, we both made a joke of not talking and became our own little silent movie. We exaggerated our gestures and expressions; he held up the chopsticks in bafflement – *What can these be?* – and mimed conducting an orchestra.

Over dinner, he asked how I'd gotten so far behind on submissions.

I hadn't wondered how – it just seemed to happen – but now I tried to think. I told him that I wasn't liking anything I read, which made me think it was me and not the manuscripts. 'So I reread everything,' I said. 'And I can't reject anything.' It was the truth, and a relief to know it.

'Did this start after you found out about your dad?' he asked.

I shrugged; it seemed wrong to blame it on that, especially since my father had never used his illness as an excuse.

He said, 'It's perfectly natural to doubt your judgment about doubting your judgment.'

Back in his den, he said, 'Let's see what you're reading.'

I handed him *Deep South*. 'I don't even know what this is about, except bugs,' I said. 'I keep rereading the first chapter.'

He looked at the first page. 'It's about a writer who wants to be the next Faulkner.'

'I got that much,' I said. 'But what if he is the next Faulkner?'

'He ain't,' Archie said, turning a page.

'But I can't just say that,' I told him. 'I think Mimi wants me to write reader's reports.'

'These are for Mimi?' he said.

I nodded.

'All of them?'

I nodded.

He looked at me, and I could see that he understood what I hadn't wanted to tell him.

'Write: "This guy wants to be the next Faulkner, and maybe he is, but I can't get past the first chapter."'

'That's all I have to say?' I asked. 'And I can stop reading it?'

'Yes, dear,' he said, handing the manuscript to me. 'Let's see the rest.'

He read the first chapter of all the manuscripts I'd brought, and said, 'Nothing wrong with your judgement.' Then he asked why I didn't like each one and, using my words, dictated the note I should write to Mimi.

Without a word about my demotion, he explained nuances of my position in the new H— hierarchy, describing office politics I'd been oblivious to.

'I should know this already,' I said.

'No,' he said. 'How does anyone learn anything?'

I said, 'I feel like I'm Helen Keller and you're Annie Sullivan.'

'Helen,' he said fondly.

I pretended to sign and mouthed, 'You taught me how to read.'

He had a barky laugh and I laughed just hearing it.

Then I admitted what a terrible time I was having with Mimi. I told him that she looked at me like she couldn't tell if I was smart or not, and that I actually became stupid around her.

He said, 'You have no idea how smart you really are.'

I said, 'Did you sleep with her?'

He said, 'No, honey.'

'These notes are great,' Mimi said the next afternoon.

'Thanks,' I said.

'But the reader's reports you wrote before were a lot more thorough,' she said.

I was about to say, *I'll write reports if you want me to*, but then I pictured having to read the bug novel all the way through. Instead, I repeated something Archie had said: 'It doesn't seem like an efficient use of my time.'

She looked at me as though I'd spoken without moving my mouth. Then she said, 'I guess notes are okay.' She dismissed me from her office by saying, 'Thanks.'

I heard myself say, 'No problem,' which I'd noticed non-native English speakers sometimes said instead of *You're welcome*.

Archie had to go to a dinner party, but he suggested I work in his den. He said, 'If you want me to, I'll look over your work when I get home.'

I didn't want to go back to Ritaville, and my office was fluorescent desolation. I said, 'Are you sure you don't mind?'

He said, 'Why would I mind?' He told me that the key was where it always was (in the gargoyle's mouth) and to make myself at home.

I did. I read in the leather armchair, with my feet up. I finished all the submissions I'd brought and wrote notes to Mimi. Then I stretched out on the sofa with the copy of *Loony* he'd given to me.

I woke up to him covering me with the afghan.

'Hi,' I said.

'Do you want to wake up and go home,' he said in a low voice, 'or sleep in the guest room?'

'Guest room,' I said.

Archie told me he was reading a manuscript by a neurologist, and it made him wish he could talk it over with my dad.

They'd met only twice, at my aunt's funeral and then at the shore, a visit that gave new meaning to *long weekend*. What I remembered about it was that Archie had smoked a cigarette on the dock and thrown the butt in the lagoon. I'd looked at him as though he was a terrorist threatening our way of life and said, 'We swim in there.' My voice sounded as haughty as my mother's had the time a handyman had parked on our lawn, and I'd told her, 'You can't expect everyone to know your rules.' The whole weekend was like that, hating Archie and then hating myself for it.

What he remembered about the weekend was how much he'd enjoyed sitting on the porch with my dad. They'd talked mostly about publishing and books, and now Archie realized that my father had just wanted to put him at ease. 'He was so cordial to me,' Archie said. 'If that weekend was hard on him, he didn't show it.'

I remembered my father's relief at our breakup, though he'd never said a word against Archie.

Archie was watching me. 'What did your dad say about me that weekend?'

I said, 'He said you were charming,' which was true.

*

We cracked open our fortune cookies and traded the little slips of paper, as we always had. My fortune was about the value of wisdom over knowledge. His was 'Great happiness awaits.'

When he took a bite of his fortune cookie, I said, 'Don't eat it – Jesus! Now it won't come true!'

And he spit it out in his napkin.

I said, 'You know what I've always loved about you?'

'What?' he said, resting his chin on two balled-up fists in imitation of a swooning schoolboy.

'You're willing to swallow your pride to make me laugh,' I said. 'Or spit it out in a napkin.'

I said, 'The good news is that these are the last manuscripts from my archive.'

I said, 'The bad news is that these are the last manuscripts from my archive.'

He said, 'Let's go to bed.'

3

I once read that no matter how long an alcoholic was sober, as soon as he went back to drinking he would be exactly where he was when he'd left off. That's how it was with Archie and me.

I filled his closet with my clothes. My shampoos and conditioners lined the ledge of his tub. He stocked his refrigerator with diet root beer and carrots.

We ate dinner together every night, out or in.

Before bed, from the upstairs bathroom he'd announce, 'I'm taking my Antabuse!'

I didn't know what to say. I tried to think what the right answer might be. Then, I'd call out, 'Thanks,' as though I'd sneezed and he'd blessed me.

I knew he wanted to have sex if he put on aftershave before bed. I called it his forescent. The sex itself was manual labor.

I was there for what happened afterward – the tenderness that didn't come any other way.

Sometimes, we slept face to face, with our arms around each other; one night I woke up and his mouth was so close to mine I was breathing his breath.

The only friend I told at first was Sophie, the anti-Archiest of them all. I was afraid to, but she didn't even seem surprised. She said, 'Does he make you feel better?'

I said he did.

'He's not drinking?' she said.

I told her about Antabuse and the poker chip from AA.

She looked over at me, and thought. Finally, she said, 'But don't give up your apartment, okay?'

I told her that my aunt's apartment wasn't mine to give up, and that it hadn't occurred to me to move all the way in with Archie.

She said, 'Call me if it does.'

Archie asked if I'd told my parents about him, and I said I hadn't. 'How much longer are you going to keep me in the closet?' he said. 'It's dark in here. And I keep stepping on your shoes.'

I was going home to the suburbs for the weekend, and Archie gave me a copy of *Loony* for my father. Then he said, 'Let's go.'

'Let's go?' I said.

He carried my bag around the corner to Hudson Street and hailed a cab. He actually got in and rode with me to Penn Station. He acted like I was a sailor, shipping out.

While I stood in the ticket line, he went to Hudson News and got Tropical Fruits Life Savers and goofy magazines – *DogWorld*, *True Confessions*, and *Puzzler* – for my train ride. We held hands walking to the staircase for my track. It was hard to go. I said that I worried he'd be lonely. He kissed me and told me not to worry. He said. 'I'm the last person you should be thinking about.'

That weekend looked just like the ones I'd spent at home before finding out about my father. But I knew now what was underneath. We had lunch out on the patio. We talked and read. Puttered. We ate dinner by candlelight. We acted like we might go to the movies and never went.

When I woke up on Sunday, my mother had been up for hours, gardening. Over breakfast, she told me she was having the house painted in a few weeks. She showed my dad and me the paint chips, all varying shades of white, and pointed out which white was for which room.

'Alabaster seems too formal for our bedroom,' he said, joking.

'It is sort of pretentious,' I said. 'And coconut for the bathroom? I don't think so.'

My mother was good at being kidded; she rolled her eyes in pretend annoyance. Then she said, 'I want the house to look its best,' with a fervor that stopped me.

My dad heard it, too. 'The house looks good now, Lou,' he said, to the tune of *This is paint we're talking about*.

I went with him to do errands, and we stopped for fruit and vegetables at what had once been the Ashbourne Mall. Lord & Taylor was now a farmer's market, and the department where I'd bought my first bra now sold organic produce.

In the parking lot, I saw the Ashbourne Witches, a mother and two daughters, who still had long shag haircuts and still drove a rusted red Rambler. They'd terrified and thrilled me as a child, when my friends and I spied on them; the lore was that the Witches returned clothes they'd worn.

He thought it was as funny as I did. He said, 'I guess that's the worst thing a suburban girl could imagine.'

*

It wasn't until just before I left that I remembered to give him *Loony*. I didn't mention that the book was from Archie.

My dad seemed pleased, reading the jacket. He flipped through the first pages, and I saw at the same moment he did that Mickey Lamm had inscribed the book for him. 'That was the reading I told you about,' I said.

He drove me downtown to the train station. He kept the top down on his convertible but rolled up the windows, so it wasn't too blowy for us to talk. Mostly, he wanted to know about my life in New York. Was it getting any easier with Mimi? What did I like about my job? Was I still considering getting a dog? How was Sophie? Had I met anyone interesting?

When I got to Archie's that evening, he said, 'How'd it go?' I told him that my father seemed pretty good, a little tired maybe, but otherwise his usual self.

Archie was still waiting, and I realized just before he said, 'You didn't tell your dad about us?' that he'd expected me to.

That's why he'd had the book inscribed.

I thought aloud why I hadn't; I said something like maybe I was trying to protect my father as he'd protected me.

Archie glared at me. 'You're equating me with a fatal blood disease?'

'That's not what I mean.' Then I realized the truth: 'I wasn't thinking about you,' I said. 'I was just being with my dad.'

He gazed at me. 'You've grown up, honey.'

It felt good to hear it. I thought maybe he was right. Then it occurred to me that if I really had grown up I wouldn't want to be told.

4

Mimi came by my office and asked if I was free for lunch, and I said, 'Sure.' She was in a girlsy-whirlsy mood, and linked arms with me walking to the restaurant.

I felt like I was going to have a great time with her, and I was surprised when I didn't.

She wanted to talk about men – 'boys,' she called them, regardless of age. All the ones in her life seemed to be in love with her, except maybe her husband. He loved her so much that he hated her.

She told me that she'd recently had dinner with her second husband, a Southerner, who still called her 'Sugar-pie.' Just as sweet was the author who'd taken her to the Yankees' game last night; she hoped he'd stop by the office today, so I could meet him.

Archie had told me I could probably learn a lot from Mimi, and I wanted to. I looked at her eyebrows; how did she get them so perfect?

I nodded as she spoke, which was all that was required, until she asked me if I was seeing anyone. I said that I was, and when she said, 'Who?' I could tell that she already knew. Even so, when I told her, I felt like I'd sold something I should've kept.

After lunch, she said that she was getting her hair colored and wouldn't be coming back to the office.

I said, 'Your hair is dyed?'

'Colored,' she said. 'Never say dye.'

Following Archie's advice, I had lunch with an agent I liked. The agent had once worked with Mimi and sang her nickname, 'Me-me-me-me.'

It was almost three o'clock when I got back. There was a note on my chair from Mimi: 'Come visit.'

When I went to her office, she didn't offer her perfume.

'Sorry I'm late,' I said. 'I had lunch with an agent.'

Her voice was like dry ice. 'If you're going to be late, just let me know, okay?'

'Sure,' I said, which came out *shir;* around her I sometimes developed a no-running-water Appalachian accent.

She said, 'There's a novel Dorrie acquired that I want you to edit, Jane.'

I'd edited a dozen novels by then, but knew I was supposed to be excited and tried to act like I was.

She said, 'No one's expecting you to make a silk purse out of a sow's ear.'

I said, 'So, you're expecting a vinyl purse?'

She said, 'Just make it the best sow's ear it can be.'

I thought the novel was silk, as it was. But knowing how Mimi felt about it, I spent a whole week editing the first chapter. Before I went on to the second, I decided to show it to Archie.

He told me that I was hyperediting, treating it as though it was a test.

'It is a test,' I said.

'You're thinking about Mimi,' he said. 'Think about . . .' He turned to the title page. 'Mr. Putterman.'

As soon as he said it, I knew that he was right and I was glad I'd asked him. I beamed at him.

'You love me,' he said. 'Don't even try to deny it.'

I got lost thinking about Mr. Putterman; I didn't delete a comma without picturing his reaction and asking myself if it was necessary. I averaged about a page an hour, and the next time I looked at my watch, I saw that I was already forty-five minutes late to meet Archie.

I arrived at the restaurant, saying, 'Sorry, sorry, sorry.'

Archie didn't seem annoyed. 'I was just beginning to worry,' he said. 'Let's get you something to eat.'

Later, though, in bed, he said, 'Are you asleep?'

'I *was*,' I said, our standard joke.

'You don't want to be late, honey.' He smoothed my hair. 'It tells the people you care about that they can't count on you. That's not the message you want to give – especially now, with your dad sick.'

'You're right,' I said. I asked him to help me.

'Just think about the person you're affecting,' he said. 'Think about Mr. Putterman.'

I met Sophie at Tortilla Flats, where my ex-boyfriend Jamie worked as a bartender – just while he decided whether to open a restaurant of his own, direct movies, or apply to medical school again. We were friends now, though I hadn't seen him since I'd gone back to Archie. When I told him I had, his face didn't change. Then he looked at Sophie with an expression that said, *Look out for her.* And she shrugged, *I'm doing the best I can.*

At the table, she and I talked about everything but Archie, until our second round of margaritas.

'Since you haven't brought up sex,' she said, 'I'm assuming there hasn't been a miraculous improvement.'

I said, 'It doesn't feel like a problem the way it used to.'

'That is a problem,' she said.

Archie and I went up to his farmhouse late Friday night. I was sleepy, but I stayed awake to talk to him while he drove. He didn't ask me to play the old car games – Capitals, Presidents, Twenty Questions, or Ghost – which collectively revealed my lack of knowledge on every subject.

Instead, he asked quizlike questions about my father: what trait I admired most in him (equanimity); what expression he'd said to me most while I was growing up ('Don't take the easy way out, Janie'); what my earliest memory of him was (sitting on his shoulders during a parade).

When Archie said, 'We'll have our own little girl one day,' my eyes went wide in the dark.

*

We woke up to chilly rain. We ate breakfast at the diner and then wandered around town. I went into Fish 'n' Tackle, thinking I'd make earrings out of lures, but they were all too shiny or feathery, too lurey.

In the afternoon, Archie lit a fire. I read Mr. Putterman. He read Mickey's new book. By early evening, we were both restless.

He said, 'Why don't we go out for dinner and a movie?'

I said, 'Methinks a better plan was never laid.'

He suggested asking Caldwell, his professor friend, to join us. I made a face.

'You look like Elizabeth when she was thirteen,' he said.

I said, 'Caldwell seems about a hundred and thirteen.'

'Don't be ageist,' he said.

'He has a bad personality,' I said. 'He interrupts.'

'He's fascinating if you get him talking about Fitzgerald,' Archie said. 'He wrote the best book on Scott in the field.'

I said, 'I'll read it.'

He shook his head.

'He never asks me questions,' I said. 'It's like he can't even see me. I'm just your young thing. I'm just the blurry young person sitting across the table.'

He kissed me and said, 'You are a blurry young person.'

5

I planned to spend the long July Fourth weekend with my family instead of with Archie and felt guilty about it. I told him, but it came out so jumbled he thought I was inviting him to the shore with me.

'It should just be your family, honey,' he said, and offered to lend me his car so I wouldn't have to take the bus.

'Thanks,' I said, and told him that my brother was driving down from Boston and picking me up. But I pictured my parents' reaction to Archie's white Lincoln Continental pulling into their driveway.

'I'm trying to think how to tell my dad about us,' I said.

'How about this,' he said, and imitated me: '"Good news, Papa! I'm with that charming fellow Archie again!"'

I didn't answer.

'What?' he said. 'You think I'm *bad* news?'

I said, 'If Elizabeth was going out with some guy who was twenty-eight years older, tell me you wouldn't be upset.'

'Your father knows me,' he said. 'I'm not just some guy who's twenty-eight years older – at least that's not the way I see myself.'

I didn't know how my father saw Archie.

A few months after Archie and I had broken up, my mother mentioned a friend whose daughter was involved with alcoholic. My mother pronounced *alcoholic* like it was on the same cell block with *rapist* and *murderer*, and meant crazy and violent and *lock the door.*

My father didn't say anything, and it occurred to me that he knew, or at least suspected, that Archie was an alcoholic.

Friday evening, I took my duffel bag downstairs and dropped it by the door. Archie was reading in the den. I leaned over and kissed him and said, 'I should take off.'

He seemed confused. 'Is your brother here?'

'No,' I said. 'He's picking me up at my apartment.'

'Why?' he said. 'Why isn't he picking you up here?'

'Honey,' I said. 'You know I haven't told my family yet.'

'Jesus,' he said. 'Not even Henry?'

He shook his head and went back to his book. He turned the page, though I knew he wasn't reading.

I stood there, waiting for him to talk to me. When I looked

at the clock, it was already seven, which was when my brother was supposed to pick me up.

'I don't want to keep you,' Archie said, and his voice was mean.

I said, 'I was just trying to think of Mr. Putterman.'

He said, 'I'd like to be Mr. Putterman once in a while.'

I said, 'You'll have to stop being Mr. Motherfucker first.'

6

I was anxious in the cab. It was almost seven-thirty when I got to my apartment, but there was no sign of Henry. No note on the door. No message on the machine.

I called the shore and told my mother we'd be late, and she said her usual, 'Don't worry, whatever time you get here is fine.'

I looked out my window down at Eleventh Street. I watched a young family packing up their huge jeep and leaving for the weekend. I suddenly got scared about how sick my father might be, and how little time I might have to spend with him. I thought, *Whatever time we get there is not fine.*

I decided I'd talk to Henry about being late. But when he finally arrived, he had a guest with him, Rebecca.

We didn't talk at first because Henry had the AM radio on for the traffic report. He said along with the announcer, 'Ten-Ten WINS Radio, you give us twenty-two minutes, we'll give you the world.'

Outside the Holland Tunnel, Rebecca turned around in her seat to talk to me, and I saw that she was pretty, though you could tell she didn't think about it. She was husky with brown skin, large dark eyes, and a tiny gold dot in her nose. She told me she was a landscape painter who sold water purifiers to pay her rent.

When she said, 'You should get one,' I thought she'd caught me staring at her nose dot. But then she told me that the water in New York was even worse than Boston's as far as chlorine, lead, and particulates were concerned.

7

In a few hours, we were on Long Beach Island, driving past the Ocean View Motel, Shore Bar, Bay Bank, Oh Fudge!, and the frozen-custard stands with their blazing signs in yellow or pink. Then there were just houses and a long stretch of darkness until we pulled up to the pine trees that hid our house from the road.

My father had replaced my mother's antique, practically lightless lanterns with floodlights, and the path was incredibly bright. For a moment, I forgot about my dad's illness and was just glad to be home; walking into the glare of the floodlights, I made my usual joke, 'At-ti-ca! At-ti-ca!'

Inside, the three of us were drive-dazed. We stood in the kitchen. Henry opened the refrigerator.

My father came out in his pajamas and seersucker robe. He kissed my brother and me, and told Rebecca he was glad to meet her. He looked a little pale, but I reminded myself that he hadn't been able to play tennis since he'd had shingles.

My mother appeared in her bathrobe, her hair flattened on one side and poofed out on the other. In a sleepy voice, she asked if we'd like cold chicken, which was what she always offered.

Henry and I split a beer, and Rebecca said she'd just have water, which naturally led to the topic of water purifiers. Even though it was after one o'clock, she attached one to our tap to show us how great they were.

My father was coughing, and I worried that he had another bronchial infection. Then I worried about him seeing me worry. I got him a glass of water and one for myself.

Rebecca watched us drink. 'It tastes better, doesn't it?' she asked.

My father seemed to be considering.

'It's triple-filtered,' she said.

I admitted that I'd forgotten to taste it.

She said that I might not be able to detect the difference anyway, because cigarettes had probably killed my taste buds.

I said, 'I thought the whole point of water was that you didn't taste it.'

Henry looked at me. '"The whole point of water"?'

I got fresh towels for Rebecca and showed her to my room. We'd dismantled the bunk-bed complex a few summers ago, but the room was still tiny, and it seemed even smaller now that I had to share it with Rebecca.

I went out to the deck for a cigarette. I'd smoked outside ever since my father had quit, years ago; I was half acknowledging that I shouldn't smoke, half pretending that I didn't.

The houses across the lagoon were dark. Now that Loveladies had been built up, it felt less like the seashore and more like the suburbs. There was no more marshland, no more scrub. It was just big house, pebble yard, big house, pebble yard.

Back inside, Henry had the TV on and a seventies movie had taken over the living room.

I said, 'Henry, do you have to watch now?'

'Yes,' he said, playing air guitar to the chase music. 'I absolutely have to watch now.'

For a minute, I got absorbed in the movie – sexy girls vavooming on motorcycles down Main Street.

'Listen,' I said, 'I want to talk to you.'

He began air-guitaring again and gave me a goofy smile.

'I think you should try not to be late so much,' I said. 'It tells people they can't count on you.'

'There was traffic,' he said, and turned back to his movie.

I knew my speech lacked the power Archie's had, but I went on anyway. 'We want Dad to know he can rely on us.'

He turned and looked at me, and I thought maybe he was considering what I'd said. 'Why don't you just say you're mad I was late?'

Then Rebecca walked in. 'What's on?' she asked.

'It's either *Chopper Chicks in Bikertown*,' he said, 'or *Biker Babes in Chopperville*.'

She sat down beside him. 'Groovy.'

Her bed was made when I woke up. Henry was in the kitchen, shaking an orange-juice carton.

'Where's Rebecca?' I asked.

He told me that she was at the wildlife refuge, painting.

'She's just using you for your landscape,' I said. Sounding like myself at twelve, I said, 'Is she your girlfriend?'

He shrugged.

I said, 'Why did you bring her if she's not your girlfriend?'

'She's funny,' he said. 'And I thought it would be easier with more people around.'

I said, 'Easier for who?'

'Everybody.'

I said, '*You* don't have to sleep with her.'

'Yeah,' he said, smiling. 'Gross.'

I said, 'Does she even know about Dad?'

He said, 'Of course not.'

Henry and my mother went sailing, and I stayed behind on the porch with my dad. He read a book about how the atom bomb was made. I edited Mr. Putterman.

After a while, I said, 'I have a question.'

He nodded.

'How come you never told anybody about being sick?'

'It was selfish,' he said. 'I didn't want to think about it any more than I had to.'

I said, 'I'm asking so I don't do whatever it was you wanted to avoid. The reason you didn't tell people, I mean.'

He smiled at me. 'Well put.'

Then he took his glasses off and cleaned them, which was

what he did when he was organizing his thoughts. He told me that the main reason was that he didn't want people treating him like a sick person instead of who he was.

That's what made me tell him about Archie.

He didn't seem upset. He told me he was glad I had someone to lean on. That was important, he said.

Then he went back to the bomb, and I to Mr. Putterman.

We had dinner on the porch, steamed lobster and mussels, white corn on the cob, tomatoes, and fresh bread.

Rebecca was back by then, washing up for dinner.

Henry sat next to me at the table. He nodded at the bowl of mussels and said in a low voice, 'Vaginas of the sea.' I looked at them and saw what he meant.

My mother served. 'Everything's local except the lobsters,' she said.

'The mussels are local?' Rebecca said. 'Is the water here really that clean?'

'I'm sure it's fine,' my mother said in a breezy voice.

She passed the bowl of little vaginas to me, and I said, 'No, thanks.'

'Jane.' My mother was annoyed. 'The mussels are delicious.'

We stopped talking for a few minutes, and there was only the sound of cracking shells and then my father's cough, and I wondered if this was why my mother was tense. 'Great corn,' I said to her.

My father asked how Rebecca's painting had gone, and she said, 'Great.'

'I'd love to see,' my mother said.

Rebecca said, 'When I finish it.'

After dinner, my father said he was tired. My mother followed him into the bedroom, and I heard her say, 'Marty? Can I get you anything, sweetheart?'

8

I woke up early. I found my mother crying in the kitchen. She'd always been a big weeper; there were balled-up Kleenexes in the pockets of every one of her bathrobes and coats. In the past, I'd teased her about it. We all had. But now I thought of the times she must have been crying about my father and couldn't tell anyone about it. I put my arms around her.

She said that my father had a high fever and his cough was worse; he was talking to Dr. Wischniak on the phone now.

As I got dressed, I could hear him in the next room, not words, but the tone; he spoke as though consulting another doctor about a patient they had in common.

When my mother told me that Dr. Wischniak wanted them to go back to Philadelphia to get an X ray, I said, 'I'm going to wake Henry.'

She didn't answer.

I said, 'I think he'd want me to.'

'Okay,' she said, though I could tell she wished I wouldn't.

We had breakfast out on the porch. Henry entertained us with stories about his boss, Aldo, who was a great architect from Italy. Aldo kept opera playing in the office all day, which Henry said made everything seem grand and dramatic.

To demonstrate, Henry composed an opera about calling his mechanic: 'The transmission?' he sang in a baritone. 'No! No! No! That cannot be!'

My father urged me to stay at the shore and enjoy the rest of the weekend. 'I'm going with you,' I said. 'You need me to drive.'

He said, 'Mom can drive me.'

I said, 'Has Mom driven you anywhere lately?' I reminded him that she drove the car like it was a bicycle, pushing the gas, then coasting until she slowed down, then the gas again.

'Oh, stop,' my mother said.

She was showing Henry what was in the refrigerator for

lunch and dinner when Rebecca came into the living room.

'Dr. Rosenal isn't feeling well,' my mother explained to her. 'I think he'll be more comfortable at home.'

'Did he eat those mussels?' she asked.

My mother said, 'It is not the mussels.'

I felt sorry for Rebecca then, being in our house and not knowing what was really going on.

At the door, my father shook Rebecca's hand and said, 'I hope I'll have a chance to see you again.'

For a second, I thought he meant, *If I live*, but then I snapped out of it. 'Me, too,' I said. 'Thanks for the great water.'

Henry said, 'Call me.'

The X ray was clear, but Eli – Dr. Wischniak – had a tank of oxygen delivered to our house, just in case. It was the size of a small child, and stood by the bed.

My father seemed glad to be at home, in the suburbs. The house was old stone and sturdy, cool inside and pretty. Because they'd lived there for so many years, they had everything just as they wanted it. As soon as my father got into bed, under the fresh white sheets and blue cotton blanket, he seemed better.

I said so to my mother.

'I'm so glad I had the house painted,' she said. 'I think it really makes a difference.'

'It does,' I said, though I wasn't sure exactly what I was agreeing with.

By dinner, my father's fever was down, and he was making jokes. When he took a sip of water, he said, 'Louise, this water isn't triple-filtered.'

I rented the kind of action-adventure movie he liked. In the middle, Henry called. My father motioned for me to stop the video, and as I did, I said, 'Freeze, asshole.'

My dad exhaled a little laugh.

When I got on the phone, Henry said, 'Is Dad really okay?'

'He really is,' I said.

9

Before bed, I called Archie. He didn't answer. For a second, I worried that he was drinking. But it was the Fourth of July, and I reminded myself that he'd said he might go to Mickey's roof to see the fireworks. Or he could be napping. Maybe he went out for a walk. But I caught myself on that one; Archie didn't take walks.

On the train to New York, I tried to remember the last time I'd heard him say, 'I'm taking my Antabuse!' I realized that I'd never actually seen him swallow a pill.

I went to my aunt's apartment instead of his. It was musty, and I opened all the windows. Then I went into my aunt's study and called him.

I listened for alcohol in his voice, but I didn't hear any. I repeated what my father had said about being glad I had Archie to lean on, and he said, 'Told you.'

I hadn't brought up drinking since he'd told me he'd quit. I felt like I couldn't, which seemed to prove its proximity. I said, 'You didn't drink while I was away, did you?'

'If you have to ask,' he said, 'don't ask.' Then: 'I don't think I've given you any reason to doubt me.'

'That's true,' I said.

'Well,' he said, 'get over here.' And I went.

10

I finally finished Mr. Putterman and read it over one more time, thinking of it as the test it was. Afterward, I realized I was more nervous about Archie's reaction than Mimi's, which seemed wrong. I decided to give it to her, without showing Archie first.

She read it overnight, and called me into her office the next afternoon. She held up her perfume and I submitted my wrists.

'This is really fine work, Jane,' she said.

I said, 'Thanks.'

'Where's the letter?' she said.

'The letter?'

Slowly, she said, 'The letter to Putterman.'

I thought, *You even want me to write the letter you'll sign?*

She went on explaining that the letter to the author should describe the changes 'we'd' made to the novel, as well as 'our' enthusiasm for the project.

'Almost finished,' I said, and took the manuscript back.

Really fine work, I said to myself on my way home to Archie's. *Really fine work*.

After dinner, I gave the manuscript to him to read. He took it right up to his study. When he came down, he said, 'It looks good, honey.'

I said, 'I need to know if you think I will ever be really good at this.'

He seemed to be considering.

I said, 'I need to know if you think I can ever be a fucking great editor.'

'Yes,' he said. 'I think you are fucking a great editor.'

I glared at him. There were a dozen cruel remarks I could've made.

He said, 'Your aunt Rita always said that the best editors were invisible.' Editors worked behind the scenes, he said; it wasn't a job you did for praise or glory – that belonged to the writer.

'You get glory,' I said.

'Inadvertently,' he said.

I said, 'Isn't that what you'd call "understated self-inflation"?'

He looked at me.

I said, 'I don't think there's anything wrong with glory.'

He said, 'Join a brass band.'

'Shut up,' I said.

'Snappy retort,' he said, and got up to do the dishes.

In bed, in the dark, he whispered, 'I'm sorry I was so hard on you.' Then: 'You need approval a little too badly, honey.'

'I know,' I said.

He said, 'But you really did do a fine job for old Mr. Putterman.'

I said, 'Mimi said, "*Really* fine."'

He turned and faced me. 'You gave it to Mimi before showing it to me?'

'Yes,' I said.

He sat up and turned his back to me, and lit a cigarette. 'Why would you do that?' he said, and his tone put me in the third person.

'What you said – I need your approval too much.' I lit a cigarette myself and said, 'I was relying too much on your judgment.'

I could tell how angry he was by how he smoked – deep drags with too brief intermissions. 'I rely on *your* judgment,' he said. 'I ask you to read *my* editorial letters.'

'You don't need me to, though,' I said.

'Of course I do,' he said.

I said, 'But if I wasn't around to read them, you'd be fine.'

He said, 'You planning on going somewhere?'

Mimi called me into her office. 'You did a wonderful job on the novel,' she said. 'But I am a little surprised that it took you as long as it did.'

'Oh,' I said. I thought of the time my Girl Scout leader told me that I hadn't earned enough badges; she'd said, 'You have to work at scouting, Janie.'

Mimi said, 'I didn't mention it yesterday because I didn't want to diminish the work you'd done. I probably wouldn't mention it at all,' she said, 'if you didn't also take so long reading submissions.'

She was looking at me and I knew that she was expecting a pledge of future speed.

But I just said, 'Yeah.' And, 'Yeah,' again. Even to myself, I sounded like somebody who smoked cigarettes in front of the drugstore all day.

I was sulking in my office, when my mother called. She never called in the middle of the day, so when she said, 'How are you?' I said, 'What's wrong?'

She said, 'Everything's fine.' Then she told me that my father had pneumonia and had been admitted to the hospital.

Mimi told me to take as much time as I needed.

Archie left work and met me at his house. He sat on the bed while I packed. 'It's going to be hard in Philadelphia,' he said. 'I don't want you worrying about us.'

In the cab to the station, he told me that when he was growing up he'd see a look of pleasure cross his mother's face and ask what she was thinking; she'd say, *I was just thinking of your father*. 'That's how I want us to be,' Archie said.

I smiled.

'What?'

I said, 'I was just thinking of your father.'

II

I asked my mother when Henry was coming. We were in the car, on our way to the hospital.

She didn't answer.

'Mom?' I said.

'Yes?'

'When's Henry coming in?'

She said that he had a wedding to go to on the Cape that Saturday, and he'd come either before or after.

'Are you tired?' I asked.

She nodded.

At red lights, she stopped, coasted, stopped, coasted. I was getting carsick. 'Do you want me to drive?' I asked.

'I can drive,' she said. But she pulled over and got out, so I could take her place at the wheel.

My father had plastic oxygen tubes in his nose. He didn't smile when he saw me. 'Hello, love,' he said.

I bent down to kiss his forehead.

He was in a VIP suite, which had wall-to-wall carpeting, a minirefrigerator, and velvety wallpaper. 'This is a brothel,' I said.

He said, 'Don't tell Mom.'

Out in the hall, I saw Dr. Wischniak and asked when my dad would be going home.

He said, 'I can't answer that yet.'

I said, 'Is my father dying?'

He looked at me steadily. 'We're all dying, Jane.'

In bed, in my old room, I panicked the way I had as a child when my parents had gone out for the evening and the house seemed unprotected and great danger imminent; I'd picture a lion slinking past the den where the baby-sitter watched television or imagine a murderer lurking outside my open door. I'd whisper, 'It's never been anything before.'

I said those words now.

All through the day, my father's doctor friends visited, in their white coats. They sat on his bed and patted the blanket where his legs were. My dad asked them questions about their children – 'How's Amy liking Barnard?' or 'What's Peter up to this summer?' – trying to make them comfortable.

When he asked how my job was, I said, 'Okay.'

'Really?' he said.

'No,' I said. I told him that I wasn't sure I belonged in publishing. 'I'm getting worse instead of better.'

'You keep talking about whether you're good at this or not,' he said. 'The real question is, do you enjoy it?'

'I might hate it,' I said.

He reminded me that I loved books.

'I don't read books,' I said. 'I read manuscripts that aren't good enough to become books.'

'What do you think you'd like to do instead?' he asked.

I said that I'd been thinking about writing a series of pamphlets called 'The Loser's Guide.' I said, 'Like "The Loser's Guide to Careers." Or "The Loser's Guide to Love."' I wasn't sure whether I was kidding or not.

'Any other ideas?' he said.

I told him about a jewelry store with the sign PIERCING – WITH OR WITHOUT PAIN.

He laughed.

'But I wouldn't want to pierce anything but ears,' I said. 'Maybe the occasional nose.'

The drugs he was getting made him nauseated, and my mother tried to tempt him to eat. 'What about a pastrami sandwich?' she said. 'Maybe tomorrow I'll bring a baked potato and a nice steak.'

I said, 'You always say, "a nice steak," like there are also mean steaks.'

On our way out to the hospital parking lot, I told her that maybe talking about food while Dad was nauseated wasn't such a great idea.

'He has to keep his strength up,' she said.

The way she spoke reminded me more of humming than thinking.

★

At home, we had a glass of wine on the screened-in porch, both of us still wearing our visitor tags from the hospital. The sky was the dirty violet of rain coming.

I tried to bring up topics other than my father. I asked about the neighbors I remembered. 'How's Willy Schwam?' He had a scholarship to Juilliard. 'What happened to Oliver Biddle?' His father died; mother and son moved to Florida.

The Caliphanos lived there now; they were raising their granddaughter, Lisa, because Lisa's mother was a drug addict. She was a serious little girl, my mom said, adorable in braids; she'd knocked on the door last week and said, 'I have a feeling there are rabbits in your backyard.'

'What did you say?' I asked.

'I said, "Let's go see."'

My mother told me about all the neighbors, going up one side of the street and then the other. After she went upstairs to bed, what stayed with me wasn't the good news – weddings or babies or scholarships – but the Caliphanos' granddaughter living without her mother, Mr. Zipkin losing his job, and Mrs. Hennessy getting robbed. I sat out there on the porch, with a cigarette and another glass of wine, listening to the crickets and the occasional car. It occurred to me that the quiet in the suburbs had nothing to do with peace.

12

Over the weekend, my father told me he was concerned about my missing work; when was I going back?

'I'm taking a leave of absence,' I said, deciding then. 'I'm malingering vicariously through you.'

He said, 'I'm glad.'

Then he looked right at me, and said, 'It means a great deal to me that you're here.'

★

My mother said that there was no reason for Henry to come, as long as I was here. But I kept expecting he would, and Archie did, too. 'Stay as long as you need to,' Archie said, 'but don't forget I need you here.'

One night, Archie told me I sounded vague.

I said that it was the suburbs. 'They put tranquilizers in the water.'

My mother was standing there, and smiled.

'Honey,' he said, 'I'm not getting a clear idea of what's going on down there.'

I tried to explain, but I realized I wasn't sure myself. So I called Irwin Lasker, one of the doctor friends who visited every day. Dr. Lasker was gruff and his sarcasm had frightened me as a child, when I'd been friends with his daughter and slept over at their house.

'The doctors are telling you what you need to know, Jane,' he said, and he sounded angry. 'It's up to you whether you want to listen or not.'

I got angry myself. 'Maybe when you hear about blood counts you get the big picture, but I don't.'

He didn't speak right away, and when he did he was grave, and I realized I'd asked him to imagine his own daughter hearing about him. 'It's just a matter of days, Jane.'

When I told my mother what he'd said, she cried, and then she got angry at Dr. Lasker.

'Mom,' I said, 'I asked him to tell me.'

She said, 'Irwin's a pessimist.'

The next morning, her eyes were so swollen from crying that they were almost closed. I got her to lie down and brought her ice cubes in a washcloth and cucumber slices. We waited to go to the hospital until the swelling went down.

She put on her prettiest summer dress. This was her way

of making my father feel that she was okay. But it was something else, too. It was almost a superstition – like if she looked pretty enough everything would turn out well.

I didn't know what I looked like. I was seeing myself in the mirrors of my adolescence, where I'd discovered that I'd never be a beautiful woman. It mattered to me less now than it ever had, but when my mother said, 'Put on a little rouge, Jane,' I did.

She watched me anxiously, and I said, 'You look like you could use a tall glass of suburban water.'

She nodded, not getting my joke. She stood in the doorway in her pretty floral dress, a watercolor of her former self.

13

As a doctor, my father must have known what was happening. It may have been gradual but it seemed to me that all of a sudden he became very quiet. When his friends visited, he answered their questions, and that was all.

I worried that he was thinking about dying, but I wasn't going to bring it up; I asked if there was anything on his mind.

'Yes,' he said. 'How's it going with Archie?'

'Pretty good,' I said.

'Good,' he said.

'I know you were relieved when I broke up with Archie last time,' I said. 'Will you tell me why?'

He said that he'd noticed Archie's insulin in the refrigerator at the shore that weekend. 'Diabetes is a serious disease,' he said. 'But he didn't treat it like it was. He wasn't taking care of himself, which made me think someone else would wind up doing it. His daughter didn't seem to visit or feel much of an obligation to him. I worried that you'd be the only one. I didn't want you to spend your life that way.' He paused. He asked me if I knew how long Archie had been diabetic – an important prognostic factor, he said.

I said I didn't. Archie's standard line was that Beef-eaters had eaten his pancreas.

I must have looked worried, because my father said, 'It's hard, isn't it, love?'

I said it was.

I began to notice how formal he and my mother were. She spoke to him in a soothing voice, but distantly, and he was just as cool. He acted as though dying was his own private business, and I guess it was.

Walking back with my mother to the car, I said, 'Wasn't it hard keeping Dad's illness a secret all those years?'

She looked at me as though I'd accused her of something. 'Did you and Dad talk about it a lot?'

She said, 'At first we did.' Then she told me that she'd cried to him once about how scared she was; he'd told her that he could not comfort her about himself.

I said, 'Did you ever want to talk to anybody else about it?'

'No,' she said. 'It was between your father and me.'

My mother told me that Henry might not come down this weekend as planned; his firm was entering a competition and Aldo had asked him to draw the trees – a big honor.

I realized how angry I was that Henry wasn't here, and I called him right back and said, 'You should come right now.'

'That's not what Mom said.' He told me that it wasn't just the competition, he wanted to research the newest treatments for Dad's disease; he'd read about one in Scotland, but so far they'd experimented only on mice.

'Mice?'

We had to be open-minded, Henry said; we'd given conventional medicine a chance and it wasn't working. In a different voice, he said, 'I can't just sit around waiting for Dad to die.'

'Henry,' I said, 'Dad isn't going to Scotland.'

'Maybe we'll have to force him,' he said.

I was about to say, *Force Dad?* Instead, I took a breath. 'Please come,' I said. 'I need you here.'

After I hung up, my mother avoided looking at me. I said, 'What do you think I did that was so wrong?'

'I didn't say you were doing anything wrong,' she said, in the even tone she now used with my father.

I said, 'You're not talking to me anymore.'

'That's not true.' She turned her attention from the dishes to the stove and back to the sink.

'Mom,' I said, 'you look at me like I'm the enemy of hope.'

'Sweetheart,' she said. Her voice was creamy. 'This is hard on all of us.'

Henry arrived the next morning.

At the hospital, he took over, talking to the doctors and the nurses. He reminded me of my father in an emergency; he was calm, getting all of the facts.

We went into my father's room together. He was sleeping. My mother was sitting by the bed, and Henry put his arm around her, which I'd never seen him do before. I was grateful to him for that.

My mother wasn't angry that he hadn't come sooner, of course. I didn't think my father was either. After all, Henry had done as he was told.

At home, in the kitchen, Henry and I split a beer.

'Oh,' he said, and he took a gadget out of his bag. I recognized one of Rebecca's water purifiers. He attached it to our tap, and then ran the faucet. He handed me a glass, and got one for himself.

'It tastes the same to me,' I said.

He said, 'Your taste buds are dead.'

In a Southern accent, I said, 'That girl is a waterhead.'

He said, 'I like her.' Then: 'When'd you get back with ol' Archie?'

'I don't know,' I said. 'May?'

He nodded. I steeled myself to be teased, but Henry just said, 'Ready?' and turned off the kitchen lights.

In the middle of the night, the phone rang.

I sat up in bed not breathing right and waited for my mother to come into my room.

'Jane,' she said, at my door. 'It's for you.'

I followed her to the phone. It was New York Hospital. Archie was in intensive care.

14

I took the first train to New York in the morning.

At the hospital, I was told that Archie had been moved from the ICU to a regular room. He was asleep, so I went into the hall and asked the resident what had happened.

She told me that he'd been admitted with severe front-to-back abdominal pain, dizziness, shortness of breath, intense thirst. Then she spoke in the medical language I'd become accustomed to not understanding.

I interrupted and asked what had brought this on.

She said that he had a flu and because he wasn't eating, he hadn't taken his insulin, which was a big mistake.

'But nothing about drinking?' I asked.

She said, 'I haven't spoken to him myself.'

When I went back into the room, Archie was up. 'I thought you needed a vacation,' he said, trying to smile. 'But it's kind of a busman's holiday.'

I said, 'I hate buses.'

He said, 'I have acute pancreatitis.'

'I thought it was just average looking.' I looked up at his IV. 'What're you drinking?' I asked.

He said, 'I'm sorry you had to come.' Then he fell asleep again.

I went to the pay phone and called my father's hospital room in Philadelphia.

'What's going on there?' he asked.

I told him what the resident had said about the flu and insulin. My father said, 'He went into DKA, diabetic keto-acidosis,' and explained what it was so that I understood.

I was relieved to hear him sounding like himself. 'Sweet-heart,' he said, 'this was what I was talking about.'

'I know,' I said.

Then he said, 'Did the resident say anything else?'

I said, 'Something about acute pancreatitis.'

He was quiet a second. Then he said, 'Is Archie an alco-holic, Jane?' He sounded as though he already knew.

I didn't want to answer, but I said, 'Yes.'

His voice was gentle. 'We'll talk about that when you come back.' Then he said, 'He's on an IV, getting sodium and insulin?'

'Something clear,' I said.

He told me that Archie would be fine.

I said, 'How are you, Papa?'

'About the same,' he said.

I said, 'I'll come as soon as I can.' And he didn't argue.

I met Archie's real doctor in the hall.

'You're Jane?' he said.

I nodded.

'Okay,' he said, 'now listen to me.' I couldn't tell whether he was furious or just in a rush. *Did I know how serious this was?* He told me that Archie could've lapsed into a coma and died. The doctor seemed to hold me responsible: I needed to regulate his diet and exercise; I needed to be vigilant about monitoring his blood sugar.

I said, 'You better talk to him.'

He said, 'I'm talking to you.' Then he walked away.

I sat by Archie's bed and repeated what his doctor had told me. I said, 'He wants me to boss you around.'

'We'll pick up a pair of stilettos on the way home,' he said.

I said, 'I need to go back to Philadelphia.'

'Your mother's there,' he said.

I told him that Henry had finally arrived, too.

'So, can't you stay?'

'No,' I said.

'Jesus,' he said. 'Not even one goddamned day?'

'My father's about to die,' I said. 'And you're about to get better.' I asked him who I could get to help us out, and as I said it I realized how few friends Archie seemed to have.

'Call Mickey,' he said.

'Isn't he kind of clownish for this situation?'

'This situation calls for a clown.' He hummed 'Send in the Clowns.'

Mickey arrived, wearing cutoffs and yellow high-tops. He was unshaven, and his hair looked greasy. He bent down and kissed Archie's cheek.

Archie made a face.

'I'm sorry I have to go,' I said.

Mickey said, 'I'm going to steal some drugs,' and went into the hall.

I could see how hard it was for Archie to say, 'Stay just a little longer?' and I took a later train back to Philadelphia.

15

When Henry picked me up at the station, he told me that Dad was on a respirator now and heavily sedated. He was being kept alive, but that was it.

At the hospital, the respirator made a big inhale-exhale sound, breathing for my father. I held his hand. But I couldn't tell if he was still in there.

The nurse came in with a square plastic bag of blood. 'He knows you're here,' she said to me. 'I can tell by the monitor.' Then she turned to him. 'I'm giving you some red cells now, Dr. Rosenal.'

Henry called friends and relatives, and they started coming.

Once everyone had left, I sat in the chair beside my father's bed again. I thought of Kafka's story 'The Metamorphosis,' and how Gregor's sister knew to feed him garbage once he'd become a cockroach.

I tried to explain to Henry that this was the transcendent act I wanted to do now.

He said, 'Please don't feed Dad garbage.'

'I don't know what Dad wants me to do,' I said. 'I just know I'm not doing it.' Henry took my hand and held it.

My father died later that night.

16

I called Archie at home. He said all the right things, but I didn't really hear any of them. He asked when the funeral was, and I told him.

'Do you want me to come?' he said.

'No,' I said, 'I'm fine,' as though answering the question he'd asked.

*

Sophie drove down. She stayed with me in my room, and scratched my back while I talked.

My mother's mother didn't come to our house until the funeral. She spoke to the caterers. She looked over the trays of meat and salads that would be served after the funeral when people would come back to the house. She clicked around the kitchen in her high heels and talked to my mother about who was coming and how many people and – *Remember Dolores Greenspan? She called.* I thought that maybe my grandmother couldn't bring up my father. But then I realized that she was trying to help: make everything appear fine and sooner or later it would be. This was what she'd taught my mother.

My mother, Henry, and I got into the black limousine that had come to take us to the funeral. When a woman I didn't recognize walked up the driveway, Henry said, 'Who's she?'

My mother said that she was a neighbor who'd offered to stay here during the funeral, when burglars might come, thinking the house would be empty. 'Mrs. Caliphano,' she said to me.

The woman waved, and my mother nodded.

'She seems like a nice lady,' my brother said. 'I hope they don't tie her up.'

The night before Henry went back to Boston and I to New York, I told him that I hated to think that Dad was worrying about me when he died.

'He wasn't worried,' Henry said.

'How do you know?'

'I was there when you called,' Henry said. 'After he hung up, I said that I'd be happy to kill Archie if he wanted me to. And Dad said, "Thanks, but I think Jane can take care of herself."'

17

Archie was kind and patient. He kept fresh flowers on the table. He somehow found soft-shell crabs for dinner, even though they were out of season. He drew a bath for me every evening when I came home from work. A tonic for the spirit, he said.

He invited Mickey to spend Labor Day weekend with us in the Berkshires, maybe hoping to break the spell of my grief.

Mickey told a lot of jokes, most of which were of the animals-sitting-around-talking variety, my favorite. He did little comedy bits: after lunch, he turned to me and in a twangy voice said, 'I have weird thoughts sometimes. Do you think that's weird?'

It hurt not to laugh. Finally, I asked him to give up on me for a while.

Sunday, when they went to play golf, I stayed behind at the house. I took the manuscript for Mickey's new book out to the picnic table underneath the apple tree.

I adored Mickey. I thought he was sweet to try so hard to make me feel better. But he irked me that weekend as he never had before. The tiniest things bugged me – like, his not washing his cereal bowl or coffee mug. I even wondered if Archie had noticed – and it bothered me, thinking he hadn't.

Monday night, Archie called Mickey and me in from the meadow, saying, 'You kids ready to go?' And I realized that what I'd been feeling that weekend was sibling rivalry.

18

There's a passageway connecting Port Authority to Times Square – the Eighth Avenue subways to the Seventh – and one morning when I looked up I saw a poem up in the eaves, sequential like the Burma Shave billboards:

Overslept.
So tired.
If late,
Get fired.
Why bother?
Why the pain?
Just go home.
Do it again.

Something changed then. I saw my life in scale: it was just my life. It was not momentous, and only now did I recognize that it had once seemed so to me; that was while my father was watching.

I saw myself the way I'd seen the cleaning women in the building across the street. I was just one person in one window.

Nobody was watching, except me.

At the office, Mimi told me that there was another of Dorrie's acquisitions that needed to be edited.

I stood at her desk, looking at the bulky manuscript. 'Wow,' I said. 'This is a long one.'

'The author's been calling me and yesterday he called Richard,' she said, referring to the editorial director. 'So it's sort of a rush.'

I didn't pick up the manuscript. I pinged the rubber band. 'Did you look at it?' I asked, stalling.

She turned her head – not a no, not a yes. 'Jane,' she said, 'I can get a freelancer. Or do it myself over the weekend. But it would be great if you could help out.'

It was hard turning down an opportunity to be great. When I did, I saw her delicate eyebrows go up.

At Tortilla Flats, Jamie introduced his current girlfriend, a waitress named Petal. She had a little daisy tattoo on her ankle and seemed light and sweet and sure of herself in the particular way a very young woman can.

At our table, I asked Sophie if I was ever like that.

'Like what?' she said.

'Like Petal in any way,' I said.

She said, 'You used to be twenty-two.'

'Jesus,' I said, 'Jamie must be thirty-five.'

'Twisted,' she said, and got up to go to the bathroom.

I looked around me. It was Thursday, a party night, and I could feel that bar-generated electricity – the buzz and spark of sex-to-be. Everyone appeared to be having a great time, flirting and drinking and half dancing to R & B, which I loved and never heard at Archie's.

When Sophie returned, I said, 'I think being with Archie makes me feel older than I am.'

'You do live his way,' she said. 'It's an older person's life.'

19

Archie was elated that I felt better.

On our way up to the Berkshires, he asked me to think about moving in with him.

I didn't speak.

He forced a laugh and said, 'I didn't mean you had to start thinking about it right this minute.'

Saturday morning, I felt the way I had as a child, waking up in the summer and sensing what I could expect that day in the suburbs: the dry cleaner at the back door to drop off my father's suits; the damp smell of the changing room at the public pool; the dusty shade in the garage.

Maybe Archie could sense it. He suggested we go to the swimming hole, a muddy pond he'd called the Butt-hole and had refused to go to in our last life. We swam in old sneakers.

On the way home, we stopped at the farm stand for vegetables and fruit. He made dinner and we had a picnic underneath the apple tree in back. He read *Washington Square* to me by flashlight.

When he got into bed and I smelled his aftershave, I said, 'Can we just fool around for a while?'

'What does that mean?'

I couldn't think how to say it without hurting him. 'Not be so focused on The Problem. You know,' I said, 'less goal oriented.'

'Goal oriented?' he said. 'What kind of talk is that? That's like *interact* and *lifestyle*.' He turned his back to me. 'You know I hate that kind of talk.'

In the morning, he wouldn't speak to me. I said, 'You're mad just because I used the expression *goal oriented?*'

He said, 'I don't like the way you talk to me.'

We drove back to New York in silence.

'Harrisburg, Pennsylvania,' I said finally.

He said, 'What?'

I said, 'I'm willing to play one of your stupid road games, if you want to.'

'I don't feel much like playing one of my stupid road games,' he said. 'But thanks.'

On the West Side Highway, he said, 'What street are you on?' It didn't seem strange to him that he didn't know.

When he stopped at my building, I said, 'I tried to talk to you about something important.'

He leaned over me and opened my car door.

I went upstairs into my apartment. It had that unlived-in feel. Dust on my aunt's pictures. No diet root beer in the refrigerator.

I got a bottle of scotch from her liquor cabinet and one of her crystal glasses. I went out to the terrace. It was raining a little. After a few minutes, though, I heard voices coming from the terrace below mine; I saw a tall woman and a shorter man. I couldn't make out words, but they seemed to be having an argument, and I didn't want to hear it.

I went into my aunt's study and sat at the desk where she'd written her novels. I thought I might write something myself. But I wound up just writing what I'd said to Archie and he'd said back.

I got into bed and turned off the light. Lying there, I felt like Archie had sent me to my room.

Then I heard my father's voice saying his usual phrases:
Life is unfair, my love.
I can't make the decision for you.
Don't take the easy way out, Janie.

Then he was gone. The quiet sounded loud. I got dressed and walked to Seventh Avenue for a cab. I let myself into Archie's.

Upstairs, I got into bed with him. He turned away from me. I put my arms around him.

'I'm here about the apartment,' I said. 'You advertised for a roommate? A smoker who can't name the capitals?'

'I can't talk to you about our problem with sex,' he said. 'I can hardly talk to myself about it.'

I asked him to tell me the truth about drinking, and he did.

He'd been drinking all along. He told me all the times he could remember. I went back over each one. Then I asked about other times when I'd sensed something was wrong, and went back over the years to the first time – when I'd gone over to his house to tell him that Jamie and I had broken up.

This was how I'd felt finding out about my father; it was like getting the subtitles after the movie.

Archie tried to reassure me. He told me that he was not

drinking now, and he swore to me that he wouldn't again. He took Antabuse and kept the poker chip in his pocket. But these had failed him before – or he'd failed them. He would drink again, I knew that. It was part of who he was.

20

I asked Mimi to have lunch with me. At the restaurant, she told me I needed protein and suggested I order the liver or steak with a good cabernet.

When the waiter came to the table, I told him that I'd have the salmon.

'I'll have the same,' she said.

She said that she'd come to this restaurant for lunch alone after her own father had died. 'I just sat at the bar and ordered soup.' She told me that she was crying when an ex-boyfriend from years before happened to walk in. 'He sat down and put his arm around me,' she said. 'He seemed to think I was still upset about our breakup.'

I laughed, and she said, 'Boys always think everything is about them.'

I thought, *Whereas everything is really about you, Me-me.* But I understood her now as I hadn't before. I understood that she needed to be told who she was. Just as I had.

She said that her father's death had been the hardest thing in her life. 'We are all children until our fathers die.'

I said, 'I feel sort of like an adolescent again.'

She gave me a look of older-sister understanding.

'At work, I mean,' I said. 'I've gone backward. If I keep going this way, I'll be heading down to personnel soon to take a typing test.'

She started to disagree, but I stopped her. 'I've become your assistant,' I said. 'I used to be an associate editor.'

She said, 'That's still your title.'

'I need to be one, though,' I said. 'I'm not asking for a

promotion,' I said. 'I'm telling you that I need to be un-demoted – or else I have to quit.'

Her face was even paler than usual, which I hadn't thought possible. I could see the blue of a vein just under her eye. 'You haven't exactly proven yourself.'

'I know,' I said. 'You're right.'

'I have to think about this,' she said.

I told her I was letting her pick up the check, on the chance that I'd soon be unemployed.

'You've got balls,' Archie said.

'Could you put that some other way?' I said.

He said, 'But what if she lets you quit?'

I told him I thought she would. 'I don't think I belong in publishing anyway.'

'Since when?' he said, strangely.

'I don't know.'

He looked at me as though I'd said I wanted to sleep with another man.

'It's all about judging,' I said. 'I'm not sure I'm the judge type. I might be more of the criminal type.'

'Judgment is power,' he said.

I said, 'I thought knowledge was power.'

'Why are we talking like this?' he said.

'You're right,' I said. But I told him that I didn't think I wanted power. 'I think I want freedom.'

He said, 'Freedom's just another word for nothing left to lose.'

I said, 'You're sinking to my level.'

Mimi let me resign. 'I feel terrible about this,' she said.

'Maybe I could help you find another job.'

'No,' I said. 'I'm quitting publishing cold turkey.'

She said, 'I feel the way I did when my first husband left me.'

This was a story I wanted to hear.

'He thought he was gay,' she said. 'It wasn't enough for him to leave me, he had to leave my whole sex.'

'Was he gay?' I asked.

'Of course he was.'

I said, 'But you said "he thought he was gay."'

'I think you're missing my point, Jane.'

We agreed that I would leave in two weeks.

I heard Archie turn the key in the door.

He kissed me and said, 'What's the matter?'

'Nada thing,' I said. 'I was let quit.'

He said, 'Oh, honey,' as though I'd made a terrible mistake.

'Don't say it like that,' I said. 'I'm about to embark on an exciting career as a temp.'

'No,' he said, and he snapped his fingers. 'You'll come work for me at K—. And be a real associate editor.'

I said, 'I could bring you up on charges for that.'

'What?'

'Work harassment in the sexual place.'

On my last day of work, I went by Mimi's office to say good-bye. 'There's something I've been wanting to ask you,' I said.

'Of course,' she said.

'How do you get your eyebrows so perfect?'

'Carmen,' she said, and she wrote down the number of her eyebrowist. Then she sprayed perfume on my wrists one last time, and I was out.

On the subway home, I got a little scared. I remembered the phrase *career suicide*. But then I thought, *Good-bye, cruel job*.

The following Monday, I went to the temp place. I aced my typing test. I soared through spelling and grammar. I was sent to the benefits department of a bank, where I typed numbers into a computer and answered the phone.

'Today was the first day of the rest of my life,' I told Archie when I got home. 'It was okay. I think the second day of the rest of my life will be better.'

He tried to smile, but it was just a shape his mouth made.

While I was cooking dinner, I found Motown on the radio and danced around the kitchen.

'What is this?' he asked, as though he'd caught me reading a comic book.

I sang along to the music: 'I'll take you there.'

He said, 'I live with a teenager.'

'Why are you so upset?' I asked him in bed.

He said, 'I don't know,' and I realized I'd never heard him say these words before. 'I wanted to help you, and now I can't even do that.'

'It's better for me, honey,' I said, but he didn't answer.

21

The next weekend we went up to the farmhouse. He did whatever I wanted to and nothing I didn't. He didn't ask me to play Scrabble or Honeymoon Bridge or Hearts. He didn't suggest we invite the professor over for dinner.

In the late afternoon, he took me to the flea market. He ate hot dogs at the concession stand and read the newspaper while I hunted for treasures. When I showed him what I'd bought – cardboard farm animals with wooden stands – he said, 'How did we live without these before?'

Saturday night, we lay outside on the grass. The moon lit up the meadow and the stars were out. It must've been their brightness that made me remember a radio jingle from when I was growing up, and I sang it to Archie: 'Everything's brighter at Ashbourne Mall.'

He got the tune right away, and sang, 'Ashbourne Mall.'

After a while, he said, 'Honey.'

'Yes, honey,' I said.

He put a little box in my hand. I looked at it. It was that robin's-egg blue from Tiffany. I opened the blue box, and there was a velvet one inside, and I opened that. I looked at the ring. It was platinum with one diamond. It was just the ring I would've wanted, if I'd wanted a ring from him.

I said, 'It's beautiful.'

He heard the remorse in it. 'Oh,' he said, 'I see.'

I was about to say, *I can't make a big decision right now – I can barely trust myself to decide what earrings to wear.* But I said, 'I'm sorry, honey.'

He spoke softly. 'I knew you wouldn't marry me when you didn't ask me to the funeral.'

My father was gone. I felt I couldn't lose anything else, but just then I realized I already had: I'd lost the hope that I would ever be loved in just that way again.

I walked through the meadow. I sat at the picnic table. I looked hard at everything, so I wouldn't forget. Then I picked an apple from the tree for the ride home.

In the car, Archie said that it was hard letting me go; I was probably the last shot he'd have to start a new life.

I started to disagree, but he got angry. 'Jesus,' he said. 'At least pretend the idea of me with another woman is still hard for you.'

'Harrisburg, Pennsylvania?' I said.

He said, 'Albany, New York.'

When he pulled up to my apartment, I said, 'You don't want me to come over and get my stuff?'

'No,' he said. 'I don't.'

I was a little afraid of him just then.

Then he reached over and took my hand. We sat like that,

in front of my building, for what felt like a long time. Then he hugged me, and said, 'My little rhesus monkey.'

Archie waited a week to call me. He said I could come over and get my things anytime I wanted to.

I said, 'I'll come over tomorrow morning.'

'You don't want me to be here,' he said.

'I think it would be easier,' I said.

'It shouldn't be easy,' he said. I knew he was right, and I was about to say so, when he added, 'Don't take the easy way out, Janie.'

'You can't do that,' I said. 'It's a violation of the Versailles Treaty.'

'Well,' he said, 'according to the Geneva Convention, I get to say good-bye to you.'

Instead of taking the key from the gargoyle's mouth, I rang the bell.

He opened the door. 'Hello, honey,' he said.

'Hi.' In the foyer, I saw my clothes and books in beige plastic bags that had once delivered our *Chinois*. My cardboard farm animals grazed on a box of my books.

'Can you stay for a minute?' he said, and I said, 'Sure.'

I saw white freesia on the dining-room table. He poured a diet root beer for me.

We went to the den, and he sat in his big leather armchair. He said, 'I'm afraid Mickey's in shock about us. He said he feels like his parents got divorced.'

'I think the important thing is that he doesn't blame himself,' I said.

Archie didn't smile. 'He'd like you to call him.'

'I will,' I said.

'He asked me why we broke up, and I couldn't explain it to him.'

I was about to say, *Honey*, but I said, 'Archie.'

'Yes, Jane,' he said, hurting me exactly how I'd hurt him.

'Are you asking me to explain?' I said.

'I guess I am,' he said.

As gently as I could, I told him what I'd figured out about us. He nodded, and I went on, saying what I thought was wrong and why. When I told him that we couldn't talk openly to each other, I realized that I was now. It made me wonder if we really did have to break up.

But then he interrupted: 'I guess I don't need to hear all this.'

'Okay,' I said. 'Just tell Mickey we couldn't make each other happy.'

He said, 'Coleridge said that happiness is just a dog sunning itself on a rock. We're not put on this earth to be happy. We're here to experience great things.'

I said, 'I don't think you want to tell Mickey we couldn't make each other experience great things.'

'Is that what this about?' he said. 'Sex?'

'Why are you badgering me?' I asked.

He smiled. 'I thought if we had a good fight,' he said, 'we could make up.'

I shook my head, and he stood up, so I could.

He helped me carry the bags outside, and hailed a cab for me.

He said, 'You going to be okay on the other end?'

I said I would.

22

I saw Archie once more. I spotted him near Sheridan Square, waiting for the light to change with a pretty young woman, pink-cheeked from the cold – a good girl in a camel-hair coat. I couldn't guess her age – I'd lost that ability from being with Archie – but I knew she was even younger than I'd been when we were together. I'd always imagined that he'd wind up with someone closer to his age, just as I would. So it threw me. And for a second, I saw them as the world-weary world did: older man seeks younger woman.

I wondered if they were married. Watching them, I decided they weren't. They were courting each other. Trying to make each other laugh. He had his arm around her, and she was looking up at him. He was a sly boots, but I could tell how badly she wanted his approval. She reminded me of myself, of course.

Crossing the street, he saw me. He smiled, I thought, sadly. It seemed like he might walk past me on the sidewalk, but he stopped, and said, 'Hey kiddo,' and kissed my cheek.

'This is my daughter, Elizabeth.'

I acted as though I'd known who she was.

'Hi,' she said. She seemed even younger than her young self, fidgeting with a white mohair glove.

Archie asked me if I was still temping, and I admitted that I was a semi-perm at an ad agency.

She was looking from Archie to me, maybe wondering who I was – or had been – to her father.

I asked how Mickey was. 'Tired,' Archie said; he'd just delivered his new book.

'The Mickey I met that time?' Elizabeth asked.

Archie said, 'Right,' and told his daughter and me that the new book, about a baker-bookie, was called *Dough*.

It occurred to me that I would have been Elizabeth's stepmother. I wanted to ask her about herself, what she did and where she lived, but I could see that Archie wanted to go. She could, too, and was taking her cues from him.

She must have felt me watching her walk away, though. At the corner, she turned around and flashed me a gloved peace sign.

I peaced her back. Then they were gone.

POCKET PENGUINS

1. Lady Chatterley's Trial
2. **Eric Schlosser** Cogs in the Great Machine
3. **Nick Hornby** Otherwise Pandemonium
4. **Albert Camus** Summer in Algiers
5. **P. D. James** Innocent House
6. **Richard Dawkins** The View from Mount Improbable
7. **India Knight** On Shopping
8. **Marian Keyes** Nothing Bad Ever Happens in Tiffany's
9. **Jorge Luis Borges** The Mirror of Ink
10. **Roald Dahl** A Taste of the Unexpected
11. **Jonathan Safran Foer** The Unabridged Pocketbook of Lightning
12. **Homer** The Cave of the Cyclops
13. **Paul Theroux** Two Stars
14. **Elizabeth David** Of Pageants and Picnics
15. **Anaïs Nin** Artists and Models
16. **Antony Beevor** Christmas at Stalingrad
17. **Gustave Flaubert** The Desert and the Dancing Girls
18. **Anne Frank** The Secret Annexe
19. **James Kelman** Where I Was
20. **Hari Kunzru** Noise
21. **Simon Schama** The Bastille Falls
22. **William Trevor** The Dressmaker's Child
23. **George Orwell** In Defence of English Cooking
24. **Michael Moore** Idiot Nation
25. **Helen Dunmore** Rose, 1944
26. **J. K. Galbraith** The Economics of Innocent Fraud
27. **Gervase Phinn** The School Inspector Calls
28. **W. G. Sebald** Young Austerlitz
29. **Redmond O'Hanlon** Borneo and the Poet
30. **Ali Smith** Ali Smith's Supersonic 70s
31. **Sigmund Freud** Forgetting Things
32. **Simon Armitage** King Arthur in the East Riding
33. **Hunter S. Thompson** Happy Birthday, Jack Nicholson
34. **Vladimir Nabokov** Cloud, Castle, Lake
35. **Niall Ferguson** 1914: Why the World Went to War

POCKET PENGUINS